Weekly Reader Presents

Mokey's Birthday Present

By Ellen Weiss · Pictures by Elizabeth Miles

Muppet Press
Henry Holt and Company
NEW YORK

Weekly Reader Books offers several exciting
card and activity programs. For information,
write to WEEKLY READER BOOKS, P.O. Box 16636,
Columbus, Ohio 43216.

This book is a presentation of
Weekly Reader Books.

Weekly Reader Books offers book clubs for children
from preschool through high school.

For further information write to:
Weekly Reader Books
4343 Equity Drive
Columbus, Ohio 43228

Weekly Reader is a trademark of Field Publications.

Library of Congress Cataloging in Publication Data

Weiss, Ellen.
Mokey's birthday present.
Summary: Mokey Fraggle has a wonderful birthday
but is in a dilemma when her best friend gives her a
present that she doesn't like.
1. Children's stories, American. [1. Gifts—Fiction.
2. Friendship—Fiction. 3. Birthdays—Fiction.
4. Puppets—Fiction] I. Miles, Elizabeth, ill.
II. Title.
PZ7.W4472Mo 1985 [E] 84-18908
ISBN 0-03-004559-2

Printed in the United States of America

Mokey's Birthday Present

IN Fraggle Rock, Fraggles have birthdays, just the way you and I do. But Fraggles can have birthdays anytime they want and as often as they want.

This year, Mokey Fraggle had decided to have her birthday on the first day of winter.

"Mokey, wake up! It's your birthday!" whispered Red first thing that morning. "Are you ready to open the present I got you?" She reached under her bed and pulled out a box.

Mokey untied the ribbons and carefully removed the paper. Red held her breath as Mokey pulled out the present.

Mokey gasped. "It's so . . . so . . . red! And so . . . fuzzy! What *is* it, Red?" Mokey asked.

"What is *what*, Mokey?"

"This red, fuzzy thing I'm holding."

Red looked slightly hurt. "It's a sweater," she said. "I've been knitting it for months. While you were sleeping."

"Oh, Red," said Mokey. "You shouldn't have done it. What a wonderful, wonderful friend you are!"

"Happy birthday, Mokey!" said Red happily.

Mokey's birthday party was lots of fun. So was the cleanup party afterward. By the next morning, all the fuss had died down.

Mokey sat alone in her room. On her lap was her new red sweater. She turned it over and over in her hands. At last, she put it on and stood in front of the mirror.

In walked Gobo. "Happy day-after-your-birthday," he said. "Boy, that's some present Red made you."

"Yes. It is . . . isn't it?" said Mokey.

There was a long pause.

"Do you like it?" she asked at last.

"As a sweater? Actually, no," said Gobo. "But it would make a great nose warmer for a Rock Monster."

Mokey sighed a big sigh. "I know," she said. "It's pretty terrible, isn't it? But how can I tell Red that? She worked so hard to make it for me." Mokey sighed again, gazing into the mirror. "It makes me look like a . . . like a—"

"Pile of stewed tomatoes?" said Gobo.

"Exactly," said Mokey.

At that moment, Red bounded into the room. "Mokey! You're wearing your new sweater! That's great!" she cried. "Now we can wear our almost-matching red sweaters together all the time."

"Oh, my. What a nice idea," said Mokey. But deep down inside, she knew she really didn't want to wear the red sweater . . . ever.

But how could she tell her best friend? Red would be so hurt!

About three days went by, and then Red asked Mokey where the sweater was. Mokey had her answer ready. "I was just about to wash it," she told Red. "I have to wash it a couple of times, because I want to break it in before I wear it."

"Oh," said Red. "Okay."

After Mokey had washed the sweater about twenty times, she began to worry. Sooner or later, Red would ask her about it again.

If she couldn't wear the sweater, she thought, maybe there was something else she could do with it. She didn't want to hurt Red's feelings.

The sweater might make a good hat.
But Mokey never wore hats.

Perhaps a pair of legwarmers . . .

But Mokey's legs *never* got cold.
Maybe it would work as a pillow.

But the color kept her up all night.

Maybe her pet plant Lanford would like it.

But the color kept *him* up all night.

Mokey didn't know what to do. She decided to put the
sweater at the very bottom of her deepest drawer. Maybe Red
would forget about it.

But Red didn't forget. In fact, she said something about it the very next day.

"I was wondering, Mokey," she said. "How come I never see you wearing your red sweater?"

"Oh," said Mokey. "I . . . I . . . seem to have mislaid it someplace. Last time I looked, it was on my bed. But now it's gone."

"Don't worry. I'll find it for you!" said Red.

"Here it is!" Red finally cried. "It was right in your drawer! Oh, Mokey, you're such an absentminded dreamer! Why don't you put it on right now?"

Suddenly, Mokey couldn't stand it anymore. She knew what she had to do. But she knew it wasn't going to be easy.

"Red," she said, "could I talk to you about something?"

"Of course," said Red.

"It's . . . something that's kind of hard to talk about," said Mokey.

"That's what being best friends is about," said Red. "You can tell me anything."

"I don't quite know how to put this," said Mokey.

"Would you just say it, please!" yelled Red.

"It's about the sweater," began Mokey.

"I know," said Red. "You hate it."

"No, of course I don't hate it," said Mokey. "I love it, because you made it for me. But it is pretty funny looking."

"I know," said Red. "I've been thinking about it, too. I hope you'll forgive me for saying this, but when you wear it, you look just like a pile of . . ." She hesitated.

"Stewed tomatoes?"

"Exactly!"

"I know I do," agreed Mokey. "I couldn't find a way to tell you. I felt so bad about it."

At that moment, Wembley bounced into the cave.

"Hi!" Wembley said. "Have you seen the bubbleball net?
We're starting a game in the Pond and . . . oh, there it is!"
And Wembley grabbed Mokey's sweater and dashed out again.

Mokey and Red just looked at one another. Then they
started to laugh.

"That's the one thing I didn't think of!" giggled Mokey.

"You know what, Red?" said Mokey later. "I don't think I'm going to have another birthday very soon. Getting presents can be hard work!"

"Yeah," said Red. "But look what a great bubbleball net we have now!"